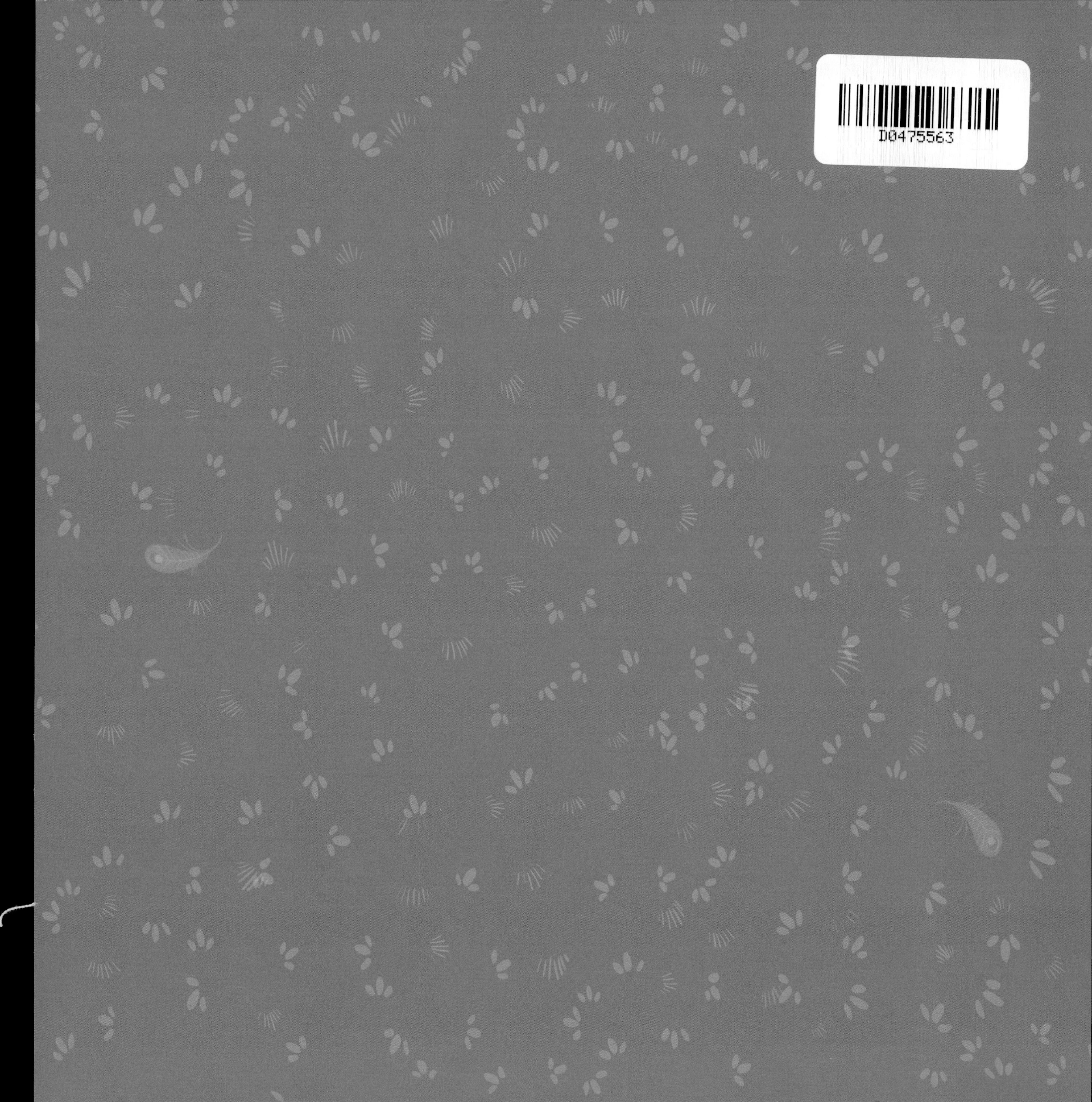
D0475563

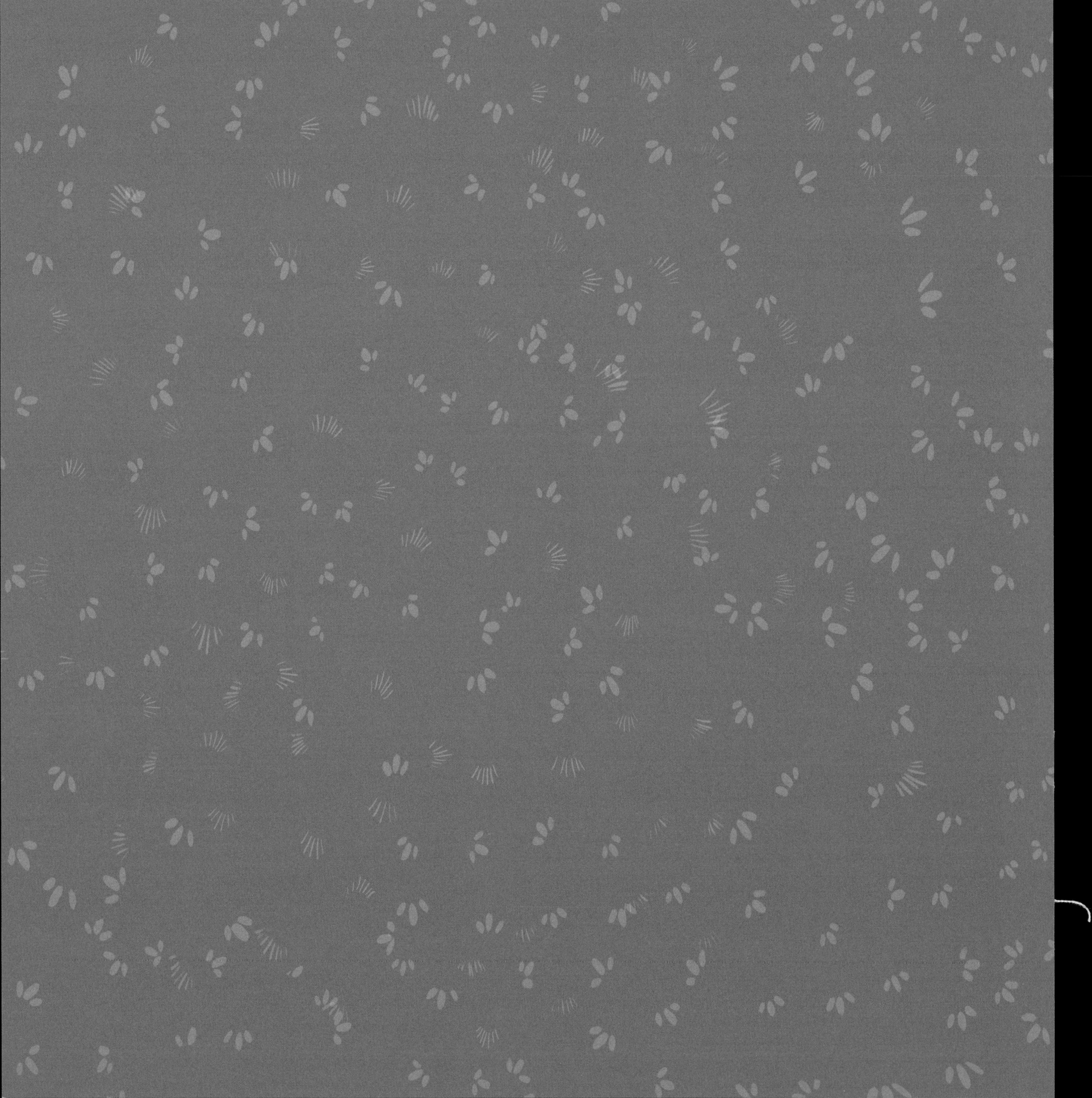

ADRIANA'S ANGELS

AUTHOR'S NOTE

Adriana's Angels was inspired by the experiences of a real family who left Colombia to start a new life in Chicago. Adriana's parents and others who worked for peace and justice in their country were threatened by some violent people. When they arrived in the United States, they asked the US government to give them political asylum. *Asylum* means "shelter." People who apply for asylum are a special kind of refugee who have to show proof that back in their home country they were in danger because of their political or religious beliefs, their culture or nationality, or the color of their skin. Just like Adriana's family, people who are granted asylum are allowed to live in their new country permanently.

Goring, Ruth, 1954-
Adriana's angels /
2017.
33305239727591
ca 01/26/18

ADRIANA'S ANGELS

by
RUTH GORING

Illustrated by
ERIKA MEZA

Text copyright © 2017 Ruth Goring.
Illustrations copyright © 2017 Sparkhouse Family
All rights reserved. No part of this book may be reproduced without the written permission of the publisher. Email copyright@1517.media.

First edition published 2017
Printed in the United States of America
23 22 21 20 19 18 17 1 2 3 4 5 6 7 8 9
ISBN: 9781506418322

Written by Ruth Goring
Illustrated by Erika Meza
Designed by Mighty Media

Library of Congress Cataloging-in-Publication Data

Names: Goring, Ruth, 1954- author. | Meza, Erika, illustrator.
Title: Adriana's angels / by Ruth Goring ; illustrated by Erika Meza.
Description: First edition. | Minneapolis, MN : Sparkhouse Family, 2017. |
Summary: Angels Milagros and Alegria reassure young Adriana of God's love as she and her family are forced to flee their home in Columbia and start anew in Chicago.
Identifiers: LCCN 2016046707 (print) | LCCN 2017005678 (ebook) | ISBN 9781506418322 (hardcover : alk. paper) | ISBN 9781506426976 (Ebook)
Subjects: | CYAC: Angels--Fiction. | Refugees--Fiction. | Immigrants--Fiction. | Family life--Illinois--Chicago--Fiction. | Colombians--United States--Fiction. | Chicago (Ill.)--Fiction.
Classification: LCC PZ7.1.G6573 Adr 2017 (print) | LCC PZ7.1.G6573 (ebook) | DDC [E]--dc23

LC record available at https://lccn.loc.gov/2016046707

Sparkhouse Family
510 Marquette Avenue
Minneapolis, MN 55402
sparkhouse.org

for BEATRICE
and
the real ADRIANA

Every morning, Adriana's angels are happy to see her.

They poke each other and grin when her little nose and fuzzy dark hair come out from under her blankets.

Adriana loves waking up to the warm Colombian sunshine. When Adriana yawns and stretches by the window, the angels think she looks like her cat, Violeta Parra.

Adriana's angels are named Alegría and Milagros. God is their boss. Their job is to watch over Adriana and help her stay balanced in the hand of God.

Milagros and Alegría like their job.

Alegría and Milagros are very tall and strong. Their heads are always turned a little sideways, to listen for God's instructions. They are good listeners. When God tells them to do something, they always do it.

Angels do their work quietly.
They almost always whisper
instead of shouting.

Usually they keep out of sight.
They do not feel the need to be noticed.

Once when Adriana was very little, just learning to walk, her brother Pablo accidentally raced his trucks over the edge of the balcony, right above where Adriana was walking. The yellow one crashed to the sidewalk in front of Adriana. The red one came clattering down close behind her.

Adriana didn't even notice the falling trucks.
She just kept walking.
The angels had done a good job.

One day Adriana's father got a phone call that erased his usual smile. After hanging up, he went with Adriana's mother into his study and shut the door. The house grew very quiet.

Adriana asked Pablo,
"What is 'danger'?"

Pablo patted her on the head. "Danger means that somebody could get hurt. But don't worry. God and Papá and Mamá will take care of us."

A few weeks later, Adriana's family had to leave their home and move far away.

They arrived in Chicago. Adriana was sad. Her new house did not have a balcony, and the winter was very cold.

When people talked, funny sounds came out of their mouths. Her mother explained this was a different language, English.

Alegría and Milagros watched Adriana sleep in her new bed. They whispered messages to her in the night.

"You are still riding in God's strong hand,"
they said. "You are right at home."

Adriana started attending school in Chicago, and now her mouth is used to saying English words.

But sometimes her classmates say words with sharp edges. “Why are you always reading?” they complain. “You’re boring.”

“And your clothes don’t match.”

Mean words are like stones in Adriana's heart.
She tries to pretend that she doesn't care,
but she does. The stones rattle around and hurt.

When Adriana has cold, sharp stones in her heart,
Milagros and Alegría listen hard to God.
God knows just how to get out the stones.

"Tell her this," God says, and whispers a secret message. The angels are always surprised at the wonderful secrets God wants to tell Adriana.

When Adriana is sleeping, the angels peek into her dreams.
“Adriana,” they say in dream language, “God loves you.
God wants to be your very best friend.”

Adriana doesn't wake up. She turns onto her side, and the sharp stones fall out and get lost among the toys beside her bed.

The angels hum a quiet sky song, and in her dreams,
Adriana sees a girl with fuzzy dark hair,
wrapped and rocked in the big, warm hand of God.

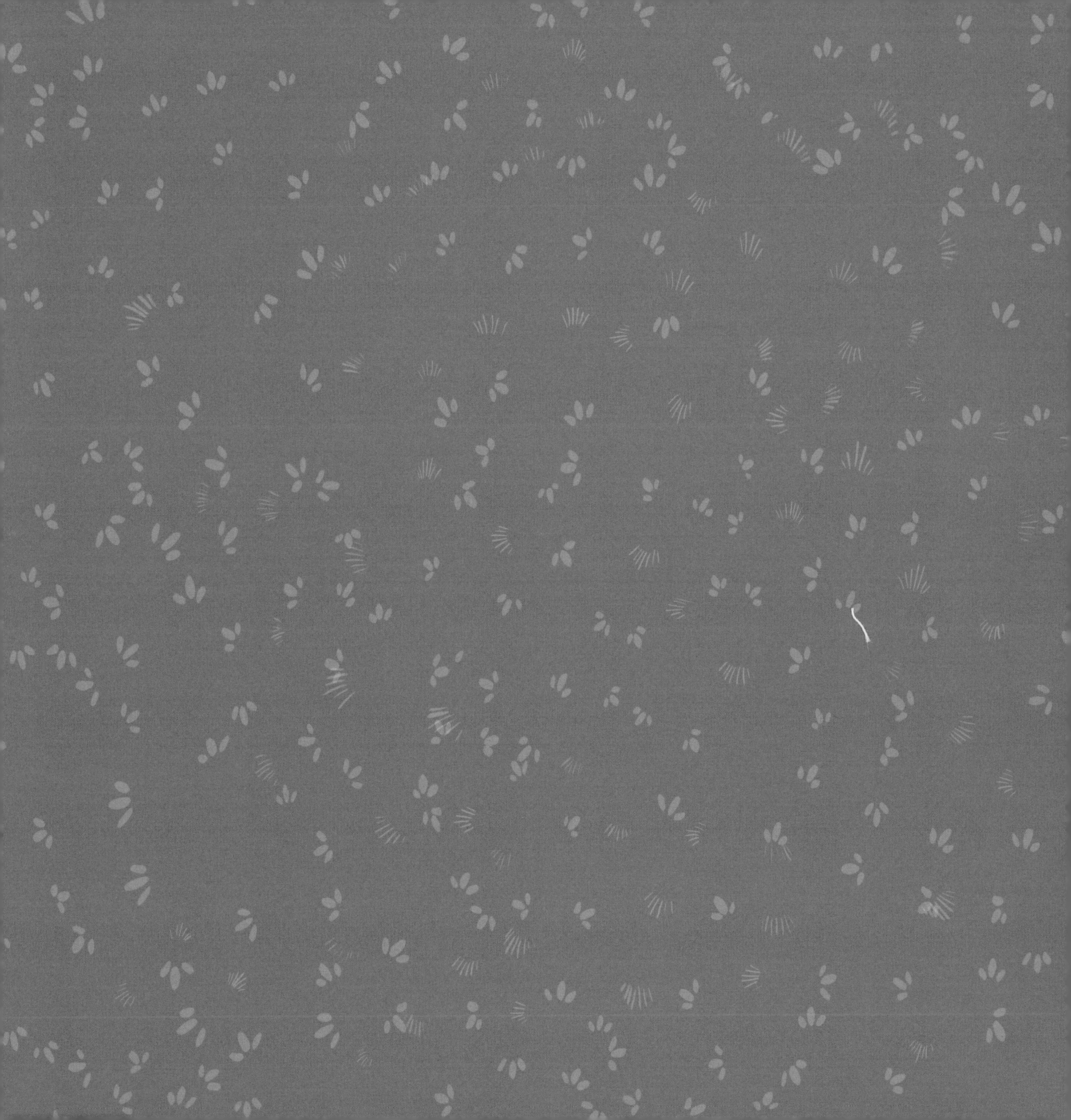

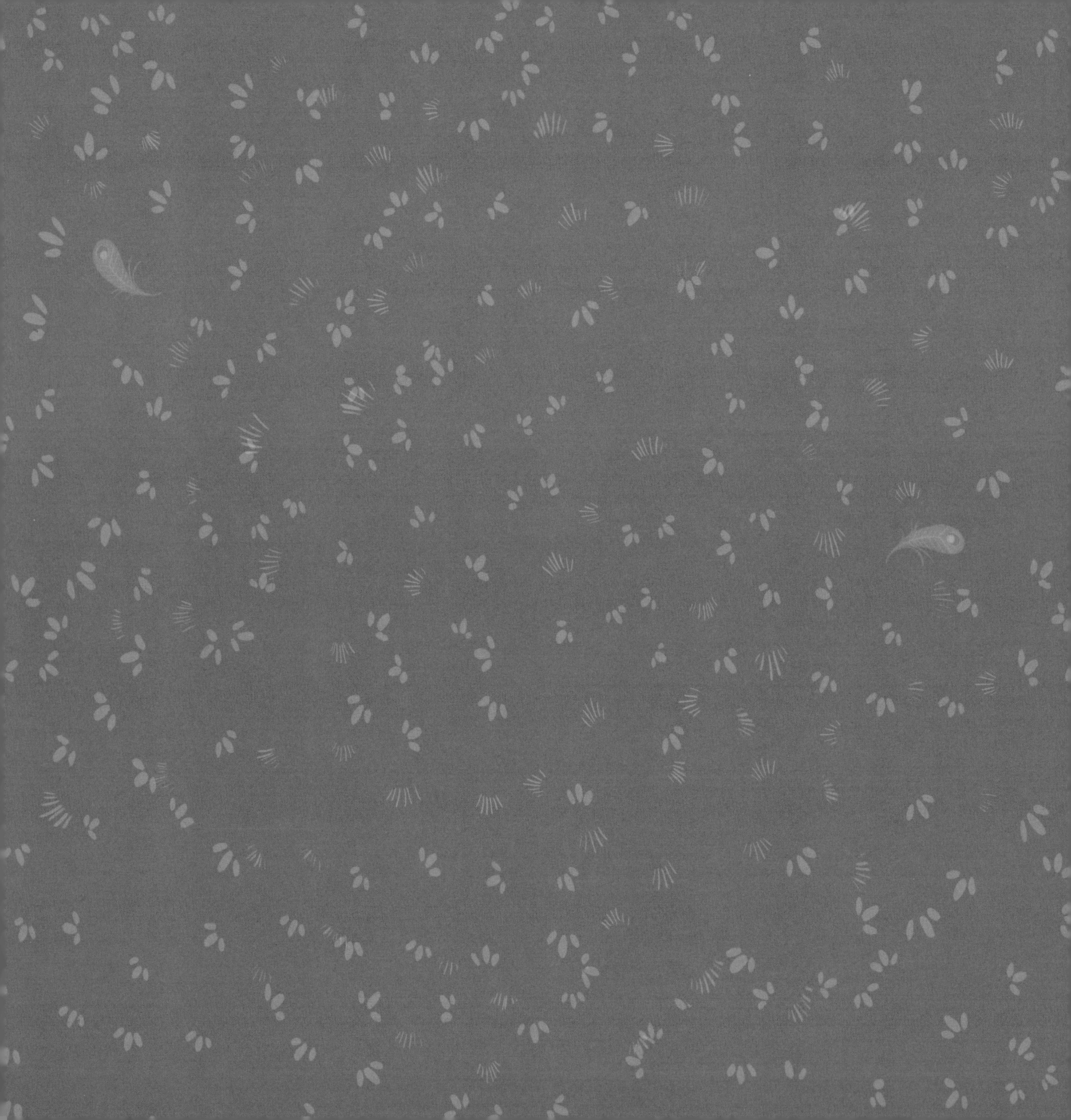